BUS SAFETY

by Emma Bassier

Cody Koala

An Imprint of Pop!
popbooksonline.com

abdobooks.com
Published by Pop!, a division of ABDO, PO Box 398166, Minneapolis, Minnesota 55439. Copyright © 2021 by POP, LLC. International copyrights reserved in all countries. No part of this book may be reproduced in any form without written permission from the publisher. Pop!™ is a trademark and logo of POP, LLC.

Printed in the United States of America, North Mankato, Minnesota

052020
092020

THIS BOOK CONTAINS RECYCLED MATERIALS

Cover Photo: iStockphoto
Interior Photos: iStockphoto, 1, 5 (top), 5 (bottom right), 7, 8, 11, 12, 15, 17 (bottom right), 17 (bottom left), 21; Shutterstock Images, 5 (bottom left), 17 (top), 18 (top), 18 (middle), 18 (bottom)

Editor: Connor Stratton
Series Designer: Christine Ha

Library of Congress Control Number: 2019955001
Publisher's Cataloging-in-Publication Data
Names: Bassier, Emma, author.
Title: Bus safety / by Emma Bassier
Description: Minneapolis, Minnesota : POP!, 2021 | Series: Safety for kids | Includes online resources and index.
Identifiers: ISBN 9781532167522 (lib. bdg.) | ISBN 9781532168628 (ebook)
Subjects: LCSH: School buses--Safety measures--Juvenile literature. | Children--Transportation--Juvenile literature. | Traffic safety and children--Juvenile literature. | Safety education--Juvenile literature. | Accidents--Prevention--Juvenile literature.
Classification: DDC 363.1259--dc23

Hello! My name is

Cody Koala

Pop open this book and you'll find QR codes like this one, loaded with information, so you can learn even more!

Scan this code* and others like it while you read, or visit the website below to make this book pop.

popbooksonline.com/bus-safety

*Scanning QR codes requires a web-enabled smart device with a QR code reader app and a camera.

Table of Contents

Waiting for the Bus

Maya walks to the bus stop with her mom. She takes three steps back from the **curb**. She waits for the bus. Safety is important on and around buses.

curb

Watch a video here!

Getting on the Bus

As the bus comes, stay back from the **curb**. Wait until the bus stops completely. The driver will open the doors when it's safe to get on.

Learn more here!

Step carefully onto the bus. Hold the **handrail** as you walk up the steps. Give other people space. Don't crowd close to them. And never push.

Taking a school bus to school is safer than riding in a car.

Chapter 3

On the Bus

Find a seat and sit down. Standing or moving around is unsafe. So is putting anything out the windows. Instead, stay in your seat and face the front.

Complete an activity here!

Keep the **aisle** clear.
Don't set your backpack or
other items there. Put your
belongings under your seat.
That way, people can easily
get on and off the bus.

Keep your feet out of the
aisle. They should go on the
floor in front of you.

Listen to the driver. And don't **distract** him or her. The driver needs to **focus** on driving. Noise makes this hard to do. So, it is important not to yell. Keep your voice quiet. And don't throw things.

Chapter 4

Getting off the Bus

First, step off the bus the same way you got on. Next, you may have to cross the street. Never cross behind the bus. Instead, go in front. The driver can see you there.

Learn more here!

How to Cross the Street Safely

▸ Always look both ways before crossing the street.

▸ Wait until no cars are coming or you have a walk signal.

▸ Keep looking and listening for cars as you cross.

To cross safely, take five big steps ahead of the bus. Look the driver in the eyes. Make sure the driver sees you. Then, get ready to cross the street. Look both ways to check for cars.

If you drop something, don't just pick it up. Tell the bus driver first. If you bend down, the driver may not see you. He or she might start moving the bus.

Making Connections

Text-to-Self

When have you ridden on a bus? What did you do to stay safe?

Text-to-Text

Have you read other books about safety tips? How were those safety tips similar to or different from the ones described in this book?

Text-to-World

Many kids take the bus to school. But some kids ride in cars. Others walk. How can people stay safe when walking or riding in cars?

Glossary

aisle – the walking path separating sections of seats.

curb – the raised edge of a street.

distract – to take someone's attention away from what he or she is trying to pay attention to.

focus – to pay careful attention to just one thing.

handrail – a narrow bar that can be grasped for support.

Index

Online Resources

popbooksonline.com

Thanks for reading this Cody Koala book!

Scan this code* and others like it in this book, or visit the website below to make this book pop!

popbooksonline.com/bus-safety

*Scanning QR codes requires a web-enabled smart device with a QR code reader app and a camera.